Inspector Peckit

Inspector Peckit

Story and Pictures by

DON FREEMAN

THE VIKING PRESS   NEW YORK

To
Lydia
my dove

et merci beaucoup
à
Trudie, Judy, et Bill

1 2 3 4 5 80 79 78 77 76
SBN 670–05101–2

Hign atop a chimney stack, a bright-eyed pigeon named
Peckit stood gazing out over the rooftops of Paris, cooing to
himself in French.

Being a clever detective, Peckit was forever seeking
new mysteries to solve. Even at this moment he was observing
a sad little girl with tears in her eyes, who was looking
out of a window nearby.

Peckit sensed instantly that something was wrong. Always eager to be of service, he flew over and alighted on the window ledge.

"Peckit's the name," he said politely. "Inspector Peckit at your beck and call. Why, may I ask, are you crying?"

"Oh, you wouldn't understand," replied the girl. "I lost my new knit bag today, and I can't find it anywhere. It was a birthday gift from my grandmother."

Cocking his head to one side and speaking in both impeccable French and in pigeon English, Peckit corrected her. "*Pardonnez-moi, mademoiselle,* I'm a Private Eye detective and finding lost articles is part of my job. Now, tell me, what is your name and where do you think you lost your bag? And what does it look like?"

"My name is Annette," the girl answered, wiping away
her tears. "I think I must have lost my bag in the Luxembourg
Gardens where I play. Or maybe I dropped it on my way
home. It's small and round and white."

While Peckit was making a mental note of these clues,
he noticed a fluffy cat curled up on the floor. "Confidentially,
mademoiselle," he said, "I must tell you that I already suspect
your cat. When it comes to small, round things, cats are
not to be trusted."

Annette was horrified. "Oh, no, Inspector! Cattiva would never hide anything from me. *Jamais! Jamais!* Never!"

Peckit eyed the cat sternly.

"Have no fear, my friend," he said, spreading his wings. "This mystery will be solved before the day's end."

Peckit flew straight to the Luxembourg Gardens and landed on a bench. He peered suspiciously at everyone around him, which is the way detectives are apt to behave. Not far away a squirrel picked up a small, round object and quickly stowed it inside a hole in a tree.

"Aha!" said Peckit. "There's the scoundrel!"

But when he peeked into the hole to investigate, something nipped him hard on the beak!

"Oh, *excusez-moi*!" he squeaked. "I've made a mistake!"

Although his feathers were ruffled, Peckit was undaunted.
Suddenly, right there on the ground below him, he spied
a small, round, white thing. Down he swooped and scooped
up a ball of string that a boy was about to tie onto a
toy sailboat.

Then Peckit flew directly to Annette's window.

"*Voilà!*" he said as he set the ball of string upon the window sill. "Here is your lost bag. It was nothing at all. Call on Peckit any time!" He strutted along the sill with his tail feathers fanned out like a proud peacock.

"Oh, no, Inspector! I'm sorry but this isn't my knit bag," said Annette. "My bag is made of yarn, not string." And she showed him a soft ball of yarn.

Needless to say, Peckit was embarrassed. Especially with that cat Cattiva watching him!

Before taking flight he poked his head inside the window and gave her his most suspecting look.

Peckit returned the ball of string to the surprised boy
with the sailboat and then flew off to a safe perch on the
awning above a café.

To his amazement, right below him on a table, he saw
something round and white and yarnlike!

With the swiftness of a gust of wind, Peckit swept down
and picked up what he was sure was Annette's lost bag. . . .

It was spaghetti heaped high on a dish!

Of course, Peckit realized his mistake immediately. Never had he tasted anything so delicious!

After sipping in the last strand of spaghetti, he set out once again to solve the mystery of the missing knit bag.

The shadows of the day were lengthening now, making it difficult for even a sharp-eyed detective to see clearly. Nevertheless, Peckit went snooping along the streets from doorway to doorway.

All at once he stopped in his tracks. There, at the entrance to a pastry shop, he spotted something soft and round and yarnlike. This time he was absolutely certain it was the lost bag. And just as he was about to snatch it . . .

up it hopped and trotted away!

"Fooled again!" snapped Peckit disgustedly. "And by a fancy French poodle!"

It was almost dark now, and before continuing his search,
Peckit decided to check in with his mate Viv. He knew she
would be waiting for him on their perch in the Eiffel Tower.
Spreading his wings wide, he floated down to a perfect landing.

There on the scaffolding was Viv, cozily resting inside a nest he had never seen before.

"Where in the world did you ever find such an elegant nest, my dove?" Peckit asked.

"It's lovely, *n'est-ce pas*?" she cooed. "I found it under a bench in the park this morning."

"In the park?" screeched Peckit, his eyes lighting up like flaming pinwheels. "That isn't a nest! It's the soft, round, white knit bag I've been searching for all day. It belongs to Annette, and I must get it back to her right away."

Viv knew better than to question a working detective. She
quickly hopped aside and watched

as Peckit flew across the moonlit sky, carrying the rumpled
bag in his beak.

He landed with a flutter on Annette's window sill, but all was dark and still inside the room. Setting down the bag, he gently pecked on the windowpane.

"Is that you Inspector Peckit?" called Annette. She jumped out of bed and ran to open the window wide.

"You found it! You found my birthday bag!" she exclaimed with joy. "Oh, *merci beaucoup*! Wherever did you find it?"

"Ah, *ma cherie*, we won't go into that!" chirped Peckit modestly. "Let's just say it was all in a day's work."

For a minute Annette couldn't think how best to thank her friend. "Here, *mon ami*," she said finally, holding up a ball of soft, blue yarn. "Maybe you can use this to build a nest someday."

Cattiva was awake now, too. "I wish your cat would stop looking at me so suspiciously," he said. "She acts as if I stole the knit bag."

"Oh, don't mind Cattiva," Annette said kindly. "That's just her natural look."

Peckit felt much better. He preened his feathers and bid
Annette *bon soir*. He even gave Cattiva a parting wink
before he flew back across the sleeping city of Paris to where
Viv was waiting patiently.

"Oh, Pecky!" she cooed when she saw the gift he had brought her. "Now we will have the coziest nest in the Eiffel Tower!"